A MESSAGE TO PARENTS

It is of vital importance for parents to read good books to young children in order to aid the child's psychological and intellectual development. At the same time as stimulating the child's imagination and awareness of his environment, it creates a positive relationship between parent and child. The child will gradually increase his basic vocabulary and will soon be able to read books alone.

Brown Watson has published this series of books with these aims in mind. By collecting this inexpensive library, parent and child are provided with hours of pleasurable and profitable reading.

Betty
The Pink-Nosed Cow

Text by Maureen Spurgeon

Brown Watson
ENGLAND

Betty, the cow, had been at Green Fields Farm for as long as anyone could remember.

Even Farmer Smith could not say when it was that he brought her back from market to lead the herd.

"Where this farm would be without me, I just don't know," she was very fond of saying. "I'm so important!"

"We work hard, too!" Billy Goat would protest.

But Betty never tired of telling everyone how important she was.

Betty was also very nosey, snooping around, trying to see what the other animals were doing, hoping to pass on any gossip to Farmer Smith. And, if there was nothing to tell him, she would make things up!

"I see Mother Horse was late out of the stables once again this morning – maybe she's feeling ill, poor old thing. More work for me, I suppose, doing her job, making sure the foal doesn't wander off."

"I was waiting for the black-smith to fit my new shoes!" cried Mother Horse when Farmer Smith asked her why she was late starting work. "Did you forget he was calling today? Betty said she'd remind you!"

But old Betty always had an answer!

"I can't remember everything," she would say. But she could remember all that she wanted to tell Farmer Smith – whether he wanted to hear it, or not!

"Baa-Baa let her friend lead the flock this afternoon!"

"Billy Goat ate some pig feed!"

"Mother Hen slept for hours!"

"Sally the dog cut her paw! She won't be fit for work, tomorrow, I'm sure of it!"

"Yes, I will!" barked Sally. "I only went across the raspberry patch to fetch one of Baa-Baa's lambs!"

But, of course, Betty did not tell Farmer Smith that. He was angry to think that Sally had been careless.

"We must do something about Betty's tale-telling," clucked old Mother Hen.

"But if we do say anything," bleated Billy, "she'll go to Farmer Smith."

"Maybe," said Sally, "that could be just what we want..."

Betty was most interested to hear all the animals talking so seriously together.

"It's hidden in the raspberry patch!" Sally the dog was saying. "Nobody will ever find it."

"Find what?" asked Betty at once. "What's in the raspberry patch?"

"Raspberry patch?" said Sally.

"Raspberry patch?" echoed Baa-Baa.

"Raspberry patch?" said Billy.

"What raspberry patch?"

Betty snorted and stamped off to see Farmer Smith. But he was already in the house, having his supper—which meant Betty would not be able to tell him until morning. It seemed a long time to wait!

So she went straight to the raspberry patch and started nosing around, determined to find whatever was hidden.

She sniffed and searched until the sun went down. But there was nothing.

Next morning, she began searching again, nosing around the raspberry patch, determined to find whatever was hidden.

"Where's Betty?" thundered Farmer Smith. "She's late for milking!"

"Oh, Farmer Smith," began Betty, "I've been so busy! I ----" But he had already stormed off in a temper.

"See you later," she heard Baa-Baa calling to Billy. "It's my turn to go to the raspberry patch."

"Not if I get there first!" Betty said to herself, determined to reach the raspberry patch before Baa-Baa and start searching again. "The beasts! Fancy them having a secret and not telling me!"

But after lots more nosing around, still Betty found nothing. "Ooh!" she burst out. "If only I could find out exactly what's been hidden!"

So, off she marched to the stables. Nobody was there.

She went to the barn – but nobody was there, either. Everywhere seemed so quiet – except for what sounded like a sudden burst of laughter from behind the hedge. Betty gave the most loud, most furious moo.

"The raspberry patch! They've waited until my back was turned so that they could go and get their treasure from the raspberry patch!" Off she went. But there was nobody at the raspberry patch, either.

By now, Betty was in a fine, old temper, nosing around among the raspberries with even more fury, when a voice thundered, "Betty! What on earth are you playing at? It's long past milking time, again!"

"Those animals," said Betty, "they've hidden something here, and I mean to find it!"

The last thing she expected was for the farmer to throw back his head and laugh as if he would never stop!

"Come with me and take a look in the duck pond," he spluttered at last. "First time in my life I have ever seen a pink-nosed cow!"

"Pink-nosed cow?" screamed Betty, almost running to keep up with him.

"Now you can see what a fine nose you really have!" bleated Billy Goat, loud enough for Farmer Smith to hear.

"Just right for being nosey!" Baa-Baa chimed in.

"Soon see you coming!" added Hen.

Poor Betty! The juice from the ripe, red raspberries had turned her nose bright pink! She looked so sorry for herself that Farmer Smith began laughing again, and this time all the animals joined in.